# Ohio
## Native Peoples

Marcia Schonberg

**Heinemann Library**
Chicago, Illinois

© 2003 Heinemann Library
a division of Reed Elsevier Inc.
Chicago, Illinois

Customer Service  888-454-2279

Visit our website at www.heinemannlibrary.com

Designed by Heinemann Library
Printed by Lake Book Manufacturing, Inc.

07 06 05 04 03
10 9 8 7 6 5 4 3 2 1

**Library of Congress
Cataloging-in-Publication Data**

Schonberg, Marcia.
  Ohio Native peoples / Marcia Schonberg.
    v. cm. -- (Heinemann state studies)
Includes bibliographical references and index.
Contents: Our earliest residents -- Native Americans enter Ohio --
Famous leaders -- Beliefs and environment -- Native Americans today --
Thank you, Native Americans.
  ISBN 1-4034-0667-7 (HC) -- ISBN 1-4034-2690-2 (PB)
  1.  Indians of North America--Ohio--Juvenile literature. [1. Indians of
North America--Ohio.]  I. Title. II. Series.
  E78.O3S36 2003
  977.1004'97--dc21
                                        2002154205

**Acknowledgments**

The author and publishers are grateful to the following for permission to reproduce copyright material:

Cover photographs by (top, L-R) Raymond Bial, Hulton Archive/Getty Images, North Wind Picture Archives, The Granger Collection; (main) The Granger Collection

Title page (L-R) Richard A. Cooke/Corbis, The Granger Collection, Hulton Archive/Getty Images; contents page (L-R) The Granger Collection, Raymond Bial, The Granger Collection; pp. 5T, 22, 44 maps.com/Heinemann Library; p. 5 Mark A. Schneider/Photo Researchers Inc.; p. 6 courtesy Tod Frolking/Licking County Archeology and Landmarks Society; p. 7 Carl & Ann Purcell/Corbis; pp. 8T, 25, 29, 30B, 31, 32, 33B, 34 The Granger Collection; pp. 8B, 14, 26, 27T, 30T The Ohio Historical Society; p. 10 Richard A. Cooke/Corbis; p. 11 Maria Ferrari; pp. 12, 33T Smithsonian American Art Museum, Washington/Art Resource; p. 15 Hulton Archive/Getty Images; p. 17 RF/Corbis; pp. 18, 36, 37 Bettmann/Corbis; pp. 19T, 41 Raymond Bial; p. 19B Burstein Collection/Corbis; p. 20 Corbis; pp. 23, 24, 27B North Wind Picture Archives; p. 28 Dave Bartruff/Corbis; p. 38 Gail Meese; p. 39T Macduff Everton/Corbis; p. 39B Marilyn "Angel" Wynn/Nativestock.com; p. 40 Scioto Society; p. 42 Ed Eckstein/Corbis

Photo research by Amor Montes de Oca

Every effort has been made to contact copyright holders of any material reproduced in this book. Any omissions will be rectified in subsequent printings if notice is given to the publisher.

Some words are shown in bold, **like this.** You can find out what they mean by looking in the glossary.

# Contents

# Prehistoric Indians

**B**efore the earliest people reached Ohio, much of the land was covered by huge glaciers—thick sheets of ice. The glaciers were heavy and stayed frozen for a long time. As the glaciers inched their way across northwestern Ohio, they acted like giant bulldozers, scraping and grinding some areas flat. In other areas, they dug into the earth and carved out deep holes that became lake beds and river channels. The glaciers stopped before they reached the southern one-third of Ohio. You can tell by the higher hills and beautiful rock formations present in that part of the state today.

As the glaciers retreated north and melted at the end of the last **Ice Age** 10,000 years ago, the carved-out holes filled with the melting water. These formed the Great Lakes and other smaller lakes. The melting ice also created Ohio's many rivers. As the glaciers retreated, they left finely ground pieces of rock which made the soil very rich. Trees and plants quickly grew in the rich soil. Animals of all shapes and sizes filled the land. It became a perfect place for people to live.

## How Do I Say...

| | |
|---|---|
| **Paleo-Indian:** | PAY-lee-oh IN-dee-uhn |
| **Archaic:** | are-KAY-ihk |
| **Adena:** | uh-DEE-nuh |
| **Hopewell:** | HOPE-well |

## THE PALEO-INDIANS: 13,000–7,000 B.C.E.

The people who settled in Ohio toward the end of the last Ice Age were called Paleo-Indians. Scientists think that these people moved from Asia across the Bering Strait into North America. At that time, the Bering Strait was a **land bridge.** These early people were **nomads.** They most likely followed herds of animals such as **mammoths** and **mastodons** as they roamed from Asia into North America. Some of these people moved into the area that is now Ohio.

**Migration Routes**

Asia

Sea Ice

Bering Sea land bridge

Continental Glaciation

Alpine Glaciation

NORTH AMERICA

PACIFIC

Rocky Mountains

OCEAN

→ Possible migration routes

〰 Areas covered by glaciers

— Present-day shorelines

☐ Possible land areas

■ Present-day Ohio

Much of what we know about the early people of Ohio comes from the work of **archaeologists** (are-kee-AHL-uh-jists). Over the years, they have collected many clues left behind by the Paleo-Indians, called **artifacts.** They have found fossils and animal bones. Some of the bones have marks that show how the animals were killed.

Archaeologists have also found artifacts such as spear points and hunting tools. The Paleo-Indians used flint—a hard stone—to make these tools. They were the first people to discover Ohio's rich supply of flint. The most famous flint supply is at Flint Ridge, which is in Licking and Coshocton Counties.

*Ohio's flint can be found in red, pink, green, blue, yellow, gray, white, or black.*

# Finding Clues to the Paleo-Indian Past

In 1989, construction workers in Newark, Ohio, found the skeleton of a mastodon while getting land ready to build a golf course. They contacted the Ohio Historical Society and archaeologist Brad Lepper. Dr. Lepper uncovered the bones of a large mastodon, which probably weighed about 10,000 pounds when it was alive. The mastodon lived around 11,600 years ago. It was one of the most completely preserved skeletons ever found. Archaeologists found flint marks on the mastodon's ribs, which prove that it was killed by the Paleo-Indians. The mastodon was named the Burning Tree Mastodon after the golf course the workers were building.

The Paleo-Indians needed to be able to follow the animals they killed for food, so they lived in tents that were easy to put up and take down. The tents had a frame of wood poles, and were covered by bark or **hides.**

**Archaeologists** are not sure what happened to Ohio's Paleo-Indians. They know that when animals like the huge woolly **mammoth** and the smaller **mastodon** became **extinct,** the Paleo-Indians had trouble finding food. Some scientists believe that as the climate became warmer, the plants that grew in Ohio changed. The mammoths and mastodons could not find the food they needed to survive, and therefore died out. As these animals died out, the Paleo-Indians also could no longer survive.

## THE ARCHAIC INDIANS: 8,000–500 B.C.E.

At the end of the last **Ice Age,** Ohio's climate changed. It became warmer, and the forests grew thicker. A new group of people—the Archaic Indians—arrived in Ohio. The Archaics, like the Paleo-Indians, were hunter-gatherers. They also lived in easily constructed tents, probably made from wooden poles, animal skins, and bark. They collected **shellfish,** nuts, seeds, and berries. They sometimes dug pits in which to store the nuts.

Archaeologists have uncovered **artifacts** and tools from the Archaic period. Many of these are made from flint, which probably came from Coshocton and Licking Counties. The Archaics also made stone axes from granite, a very hard stone. They used the axes to cut down trees and carve canoes. They made weights and decorations from another type of stone called slate. These then became part of a weapon called an atlatl. Atlatls were used to throw spears much farther than they could be thrown by hand.

The Archaic Indians were traders. We know this because archaeologists have found artifacts made from copper and shells buried in graves. The copper and shells were not found naturally in the areas in which the Archaic Indians lived. They came from an area to the north, around Lake Superior. Therefore, archaeologists believe that the Archaics traded goods for the copper and shells.

*Ohio's Archaic Indians used a tool called an atlatl while hunting. Archaeologists have learned that at this time, early peoples used atlatls all over the world.*

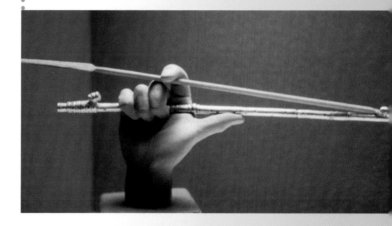

## THE ADENA: 800 B.C.E.–C.E. 100

The next **prehistoric** people to settle in Ohio were the Adena. The Adena are sometimes called Woodland Indians. The Adena were the first people to build mounds in Ohio. They were also Ohio's first farmers.

These early farmers set up permanent villages so that they could tend to their crops of pumpkins, sunflowers, tobacco, and squash. They also hunted small **game.**

*The Serpent Mound in southern Ohio, in Adams County, is shaped like a coiling snake. It is the longest mound of its kind in the United States. Some archaeologists think the Adena built the Serpent Mound. Others believe it was built by the Fort Ancients.*

*This Adena artifact, found in Ross County, is a pipe carved in the shape of a person.*

Most houses found in the permanent villages of the Adena were circular, with cone-shaped roofs. The houses were made from poles, willows, and tree bark.

The Adena made axes, pipes, and pottery from stone. Adena **artifacts** made from copper and **mica** have been found hundreds of miles from their homeland in southern Ohio. This makes **archaeologists** believe that the Adena traded their goods with other peoples who lived far away.

Mounds made by the Adena were constructed from dirt. Some are round. Others are shaped like animals. Adena mounds can be found in almost every county in Ohio. Many of the mounds were used for burials, while others were used as meeting places or places to hold ceremonies.

## THE HOPEWELL: 100 B.C.E.–C.E. 500

Hopewell **culture** grew out of Adena culture. The Hopewell are also known sometimes as Woodland Indians. The Hopewell lived in well-organized, permanent farming villages near lakes and streams in central and southern Ohio. They planted corn, pumpkins, sunflowers, and tobacco, but also depended on hunting and fishing as well as gathering nuts, fruits, seeds, and roots to survive.

The Hopewell are best known for their mounds, many of which can still be seen today. Mounds built by the Hopewell were much bigger than those built by the Adena. They often built their mounds in geometric shapes: squares, **parallel** lines, circles, and rectangles. Others were shaped like animals. The mounds were used as trading posts, places of worship, and gathering places.

The Hopewell built the largest **prehistoric** hilltop **enclosure** in the United States at a place called Fort Ancient. Over a period of about 60 years, they built 18,000 feet of earthen walls. They carried the dirt basket by basket. They used enough dirt to fill dump trucks lined up for 200 miles. A line of trucks that long would reach nearly across the state, from Ohio's Indiana border in the west to the Pennsylvania state line in the east (map page 44).

## Hopewell Traders

Archaeologists know that the Hopewell traded with people from far away because of certain artifacts they have found in Ohio.

| ARTIFACT | ORIGINAL LOCATION |
| --- | --- |
| **obsidian** | Rocky Mountains |
| grizzly bear teeth | Rocky Mountains |
| copper | upper Great Lakes |
| conch shells | Gulf of Mexico |
| mica | southern Appalachian Mountains |

*This Hopewell **artifact,** showing a human hand, is made from **mica.** The Hopewell also used copper, silver, and sometimes gold when making tools and art.*

At first, **archaeologists** thought the hilltop **enclosure** was a fort built for protection. Today, we know that it was a place where the Hopewell made their homes, held religious ceremonies, and buried their dead.

### THE FORT ANCIENTS: C.E. 1000–1650

The Fort Ancient people, who lived in southern Ohio, were the last of Ohio's **prehistoric** peoples. They are sometimes called Late Prehistoric Indians. It is important to understand that they did not build the enclosure called Fort Ancient that was discussed before.

## History and Prehistory

Europeans came to North America in the late 1500s, and history started to be written down. Any time period in history that is recorded with written words is considered to take place in **historic** times. There is a mysterious gap in time between the last of the prehistoric Indians and the earliest historic Indians. We may not ever know what happened to the last of Ohio's prehistoric peoples.

The Fort Ancients lived in permanent villages and farmed the area the Hopewell had previously farmed. Their houses were circular or rectangular in shape, and were arranged around central **plazas.** Like the people who lived there before them, the Fort Ancients farmed

# How to Be a Junior Archaeologist

You can help the Ohio Historic Preservation Office by looking for artifacts near your home. If you uncover an artifact, call the Ohio Historical Society in Columbus to get a form for recording information. In the meantime, it is a good idea to draw a map of the location where you found the artifact. Do not continue to dig or remove objects. An archaeologist may be interested in coming to the property to investigate. The property owner must give his or her permission before a site can be **excavated,** but each year new sites are selected. More than two thousand sites have been reported so far. These are usually named for their owners.

"Most visitors who bring in **projectile points** ask me which tribe made them. They are surprised when they find out these arrow points are thousands of years old, not hundreds," says Jack Blosser, from the Fort Ancient Museum. Prehistoric Indians used the stone projectiles. Early historic Indians began making sharper points from metals introduced by the Europeans.

in addition to hunting with bows and arrows. They also built mounds. Some archaeologists believe that the Fort Ancients used the mounds like a **sundial** in order to tell time. Later, however, they stopped building mounds and started to bury their dead in cemeteries.

There is some evidence that the Fort Ancients were the people responsible for building the Serpent Mound in Adams County, Ohio. The Serpent Mound is a large mound in the shape of a snake. The mound, which is almost the length of four football fields, probably had some kind of religious meaning for its builders.

# Historic Indians of Ohio

**B**etween 1650 and 1700, members of the Iroquois Confederacy, a group of five Indian tribes from New York state, moved into the **Ohio Country.** They drove out the native peoples—the descendants of Ohio's **Prehistoric** Indians—who were already living in the eastern part of the region. Those conflicts were called the **Beaver Wars,** because the main reason the Iroquois had come was to get beaver **pelts** to trade to French traders. The Beaver Wars lasted until around 1700. During that time, the Iroquois kept other native peoples out of the Ohio Country, so it was mostly unoccupied. The Iroquois used the land for hunting, but did not live there.

By the late 1600s and early 1700s, other Indian tribes entered the Ohio Country. By the late 1700s, six major Indian groups lived in villages in the Ohio Country. These were the Shawnee, the Miami, the Wyandot, the Ottawa, the Delaware, and the Mingo.

### THE SHAWNEE

Of all the **historic** Indian groups in Ohio, the Shawnee

*The Iroquois came to the Ohio Country because of the land's rich hunting grounds.*

During historic times, there were six main groups of Indians that lived in Ohio.

| | |
|---|---|
| Delaware: | DEL-uh-where |
| Miami | my-YAM-ee |
| Mingo | MING-oh |
| Ottawa | AH-teh-wah |
| Shawnee | shaw-NEE |
| Wyandot | WHY-an-dot |

may be able to trace their roots back the farthest. They had been living in Ohio as early as the late 1600s, but were forced out by the Iroquois during the Beaver Wars in the 1660s. They scattered to other states, such as Pennsylvania and Tennessee. Even after they had been turned out by the Iroquois, small Shawnee hunting parties returned to their former territory to hunt each year. When they finally returned to resettle Ohio in the 1730s, as the power of the Iroquois lessened, they settled mostly north of the Ohio River, between the Allegheny and Scioto Rivers.

# Ohio's Indian Nations

| Nation | Language | Location | Famous Leaders |
|---|---|---|---|
| Delaware | **Algonquian** | eastern Ohio | White Eyes, Netawatwees |
| Miami | Algonquian | western Ohio | Little Turtle |
| Mingo | Iroquois | eastern, central Ohio | Logan |
| Ottawa | Algonquian | northern Ohio | Pontiac |
| Shawnee | Algonquian | southern Ohio | Tecumseh, Blue Jacket, Cornstalk, the Prophet |
| Wyandot | Iroquois | northern Ohio | Tarhe |

*Blue Jacket, a Shawnee Indian, was a war chief. Some historians believe he was actually a white settler who chose to live his life among the Shawnee.*

Each Shawnee belonged to his or her father's **clan.** There were two kinds of chiefs: a civil chief, who led the tribe during times of peace, and a war chief, who led the tribe in battles. The civil chiefdom was a lifetime position, and was passed from father to son. The war chief was chosen for his skill in battle. While the chiefs were usually men, the Shawnee did have several female war and civil chiefs during the 1700s.

In the summertime, the Shawnee lived in large family groups in bark-covered **longhouses.** In the fall, they broke up into smaller family groups and lived in hunting camps. Shawnee men were the warriors. They were also responsible for fishing, and for hunting deer, turkey, pheasant, and buffalo. Shawnee women tended to the large fields of corn, beans, and squash.

In the spring, the Shawnee performed the Bread Dance in order to celebrate the planting of their fields. As the crops were growing, they danced the Green Corn Dance. They performed the Autumn Bread Dance in the fall to celebrate the harvest. In these ways, the Shawnee demonstrated their close relationship with the Earth.

The Shawnee believed that Kohkumthena, or "grandmother," watched over the world. She was a weaver, and was continuously weaving a large blanket. The Shawnee believed that the world would end when Kohkumthena finished weaving her blanket and threw it over the Earth. Good people would be caught in the blanket and pulled up to the heavens.

In the 1700s, before there were many European settlers in the **Ohio Country,** Shawnee men wore leather **breechcloths** and leggings that reached above the knee. Women wore leggings, moccasins, and a skin overblouse. In warm weather, their robes were made

*The Shawnee warrior Paytakootha, or Flying Clouds, wore earrings, a nose ring, and red face paint.*

from lightweight deerskin. During the winter, they used robes made from bear or buffalo **hides.** Their clothing was often decorated with dyed porcupine quills, feathers, and paint. The fronts of men's heads were shaved, and they wore necklaces, earrings, and nose rings. They also either painted or tattooed red lines on their faces. After they had more contact with Europeans, the Shawnee adopted a more European style of dress, keeping only their original face paints and earrings.

# The Shawnee and the Celestial Sisters

There is a group of stars in the sky that **astronomers** today call the Corona Borealis (core-OWN-uh bore-ee-AL-is). It is shaped like a circle. The Shawnee called it the Celestial Sisters, and this is the story behind that name.

One day a great hunter named White Hawk was looking for **game.** He came to the edge of a large prairie, and in the middle he saw a large circle worn in the grass. As he stood there, he saw a large silver basket come down from the sky. Twelve beautiful sisters got out of the basket and began to dance. He fell in love with the most beautiful of the sisters and tried to capture her. The sisters jumped back into their basket and escaped into the sky. The next day, the hunter disguised himself as a rabbit and tried again to capture the beautiful maiden. He failed again. The following day, he disguised himself as a mouse, and was able to capture her. He took her home as his wife. She soon became homesick. One day, while White Hawk was out hunting, she made a silver basket of her own. She sang a special song, and was carried away back to the heavens.

The Shawnee thought that the stars of the Corona Borealis were made up of the circle of dancing maidens.

15

## THE MIAMI

The Miami, who were **Algonquian** speakers, originally came to Ohio around 1700 from present-day Wisconsin, Indiana, and Michigan. They became a very powerful group in Ohio. They settled at the head of the Maumee River, and had a reputation for being polite and for dressing well.

Each Miami belonged to his or her father's **clan.** One was not permitted to marry within one's own clan. Within each village, all clan chiefs made up a council. Village councils sent representatives to a larger band council. The band council then sent chiefs to a tribal council. Each band often had two chiefs. One led the group from day to day. The other was a war chief, chosen for his fighting abilities. This is how the Miami were governed.

In the summertime, the Miami lived in permanent villages. Their **longhouses** were framed by wooden poles and then covered by rush mats. Each village also had a large building that was used for meetings and ceremonies. After the fall harvest the Miami moved to the prairies, where they hunted together for bison. They then broke into smaller groups and lived in winter hunting camps.

## Miami Games

The Miami liked to play games. The object of one game was to have one person throw an object into the air. Another person would try to shoot the object with a bow and arrow. This game helped their hunting skills stay sharp. The Miami also enjoyed swimming and wrestling.

Miami women grew corn, melon, squash, beans, and pumpkins. The Miami were famous for the superior type of white corn that they grew. They traded this white corn with other Indian nations in Ohio and the surrounding areas. Miami men were the warriors. They also grew tobacco and hunted and fished. The women then turned the deer, bear, and buffalo that the men had killed into food and clothing. Both men and women tattooed themselves.

## THE WYANDOT

The Wyandot were originally from southern Ontario, Canada. Even though they were distantly related to the Iroquois who lived further east, the Iroquois drove the Wyandot from their land. They settled throughout Ohio after 1700, including in what today are Wyandot, Marion, and Crawford Counties. Lancaster, Coshocton, and Upper Sandusky were once Wyandot villages.

The Wyandot lived in rectangular, barrel-roofed houses. Men hunted **game** and grew tobacco. Women grew corn, beans, squash, and sunflowers. All farmland was controlled by clans related by female relatives.

All people were governed by a council made up of the chiefs of each Wyandot clan. By about 1750, there were

*Sunflowers were an important crop for the Wyandot. They ground the seeds into flour to make bread. They also squeezed oil from the seeds and used it to moisturize their skin and hair.*

ten **clans.** The male chiefs were chosen by the clan mothers, powerful women with decision-making powers.

Wyandot men and women wore clothing made of blackened buckskin. Clan symbols were often painted on the clothing in red paint. In warm weather, men wore **breechcloths** that hung to their knees. When it was cold, they added fur robes. In cooler weather, men and women wore tunics with sleeves that could be attached. Leather belts worn under the tunics allowed leg coverings to be attached. Women also used that belt to secure their skirts. In snowy or muddy conditions, men and women wore overshoes made of cornhusks.

The Wyandot believed that a woman prophet, or seer, created the continent. She lived on a tiny island, and prayed to the Great Being to make the island larger. Muskrats and tortoises brought mud to make the island larger. That land became the home of the Wyandot people.

Every ten years, the Wyandot celebrated the Feast of the Dead. At that time, they dug up the remains of all people who had died since the last Feast of the Dead. Then, they buried all the remains in a common grave. Only then, the Wyandot believed, would the souls of the dead be able to go to the heavens.

*Into the 1940s and beyond, Wyandot Indians still wore traditional clothing on special occasions.*

*The Ottawa covered their domed houses with coverings of bark (shown here), thatch, or animal* **hides.**

## THE OTTAWA

The Ottawa came to Ohio from Canada around 1740. They settled along the Sandusky and Cuyahoga Rivers. The Ottawa were well known for their abilities as traders. In the **Algonquian** language, *Ottawa* means "to trade." They traded furs, skins, corn, sunflower oil, tobacco, roots, and herbs with other tribes.

The Ottawa made and used birchbark canoes to travel long distances to trade their goods. They also used toboggans, or large sleds, and snowshoes in order to travel through the snowy Ohio winters.

Ottawa women grew corn, potatoes, peas, beans, pumpkins, and wild rice. Men hunted and fished. The Ottawa also **tapped** maple trees for maple syrup.

*This painting shows two Ottawa chiefs in traditional clothing. A birchbark canoe can be seen in the background.*

In the summertime, the Ottawa lived in domed houses. After the fall harvest, they split up into smaller winter hunting camps.

The Ottawa believed in a great spirit: Kitchi Manitou. Kitchi Manitou was an all-powerful spirit who had created the world.

## THE DELAWARE

The Delaware came to Ohio in the early 1740s from Pennsylvania, Delaware, and New Jersey as European colonists pushed them from their land. They set up many villages along the Muskingum and Auglaize Rivers in eastern and northwestern Ohio. The Delaware, who were **Algonquian** speakers, call themselves the Lenape (len-UP-ee). In their language, *Lenape* means "original people." The Miami, Ottawa, and Shawnee called the Delaware "grandfathers," because they were thought to be the original Algonquin nation.

Women were the farmers, and also made pots, baskets, and clothing from animal skins. Women tended fields of corn, beans, squash, and sunflowers. In the summertime, the Delaware lived together in farming towns, in **longhouses** shingled with tree bark. Each fall, a celebration was held to celebrate the harvest and to pray for good hunting. This celebration lasted for two weeks.

*Both Delaware men and women wore leggings made of buckskin. Men wore feathers on their heads.*

Men were responsible for hunting, waging war, and for making tools and weapons. They hunted alone except during the fall, when they took part in group deer hunts. During the fall and winter, the villages split up into smaller hunting camps. The men hunted for deer, elk, black bear, raccoon, beaver, rabbit, turkeys, ducks, geese, and passenger pigeons. They also caught fish with large nets and harpoons. Sometimes, they smoked and dried the meat so that it would not spoil and so that it could be eaten at a later time.

The Delaware were taught to respect animals. One story tells about a young Delaware boy who shot and wounded a bear, but then did not kill it for food. By doing this, the boy was torturing the animal. Soon, the bears in the forest punished him. They ripped off his arms and legs, put them back on, and let him run home. His arms and legs fell off when he reached his village. This story taught children that there were **consequences** for not treating animals with respect.

According to the Delaware creation story, the land was thought into being by a creator. He made a giant turtle rise from the sea. A huge cedar tree grew out of the turtle's back. That tree produced the first man and woman. They became the parents of all other life.

## THE MINGO

British settlers had forced many Iroquois out of the New York region by 1740. Some Iroquois moved west, into Pennsylvania. Those Iroquois groups in Pennsylvania became known as the Mingo. The Mingo were mostly made up of **refugees** from other tribes, such as the Seneca, Wyandot, and Shawnee, who had been adopted by the Iroquois after they had been defeated in battle. Just before the Revolutionary War (1775–1783), the Mingo migrated into Ohio. First, they lived by the Ohio River near Steubenville. Then they moved by the Scioto River, where the city of Columbus is today.

Although the Mingo spoke the Iroquois language, they allied themselves with the Algonquian speakers they found in the **Ohio Country** and worked to keep the Iroquois from spreading their influence there.

# European Influence

In 1679, the French explorer René-Robert Cavelier, Sieur de La Salle, was probably the first European to see the **Ohio Country.** He traveled through Lake Erie at that time. He also may have traveled down the Ohio River. Ohio's native peoples had no way of knowing this at the time, but their lives were about to change forever.

## European Contact, 1670–1794

CANADA

*Lake Erie*

La Salle's route of exploration, 1679

Michigan

Pennsylvania

Fort Miamis
1794

Ottawa

✖ Battle of
Fallen Timbers
1794

Fort Sandusky
1762

Fort
Defiance
1794

Wyandot

Fort
Laurens
1778

Indiana

Fort Recovery
1794

Upper
Sandusky

Wapakoneta
Lewistown

Mingo

Newcomer's
Town

Miami

Delaware

Piqua

Fort Greenville
1793

Fort Harmar
1784

Fort Washington
1790

La Salle's route
of exploration, 1670

Shawnee

Lower
Shawnee
Town

West
Virginia

Kentucky

0          75 mi

🐾 Indian towns

## Indian Hunting Grounds and the European Fur Trade: 1680–1750

La Salle claimed all of the land he found—including the Ohio Country—for France. French traders began to arrive, but they had no interest in settling the land. They merely wanted to trade European goods, such as iron tools, cloth, and alcohol, for the furs the Ohio Indians trapped for them.

*Indians and fur traders often did not speak the same language, so they communicated with hand signals.*

The British, who also claimed the Ohio Country as their own, noticed that the French traders were making large sums of money by selling the furs in Europe. They became worried that the French and the Indians were

## A Fair Trade?

At times, relations between the Europeans and the Indians were peaceful. The Europeans were eager to learn how to grow tobacco. The Indians also taught the Europeans how to make maple syrup and plant corn and squash. In turn, the Indians learned about European grains like wheat and oats.

But not everything that the Europeans brought to the Ohio Country was good. They introduced diseases, such as smallpox and measles, which the Indians had never been exposed to before. The Indians had no resistance to these new illnesses, and their traditional medicines did not help. Many times, entire villages were wiped out by **epidemics.** During the **French and Indian War** (1756–1763), there is even evidence that the British used **germ warfare** by giving Indians blankets infected with smallpox germs.

developing an **alliance** that would prevent the British from taking advantage of the region's rich **resources.** The British therefore entered the fur trade themselves. They started to offer more European goods to the Indians in return for fewer furs, and the French lost much of their business to the British. One important side effect of the fur trade was that the Ohio Indians became more and more dependent on European trade goods. They trapped more and more animals to get skins to trade. This meant that competition between Indian nations over hunting grounds increased.

## THE FRENCH AND INDIAN WAR: 1754–1763

Both the French and the British started to build forts to protect their trading posts in the **Ohio Country.** In the early 1750s, British settlers started to move into the region. The Indians in the Ohio Country were happy to trade with both countries, but they did not want settlers on their land. They felt threatened by the settlers. Therefore, when the **French and Indian War** finally broke out in 1754, most Ohio Indians—including the Shawnee, the Miami, the Ottawa, and the Wyandot—sided with the French. Even with the support of the Indians, the French could not win the war. When it ended in 1763, the French gave up all rights to the Ohio Country to the British. To the dismay of the Indians, British settlers began to move into the region in waves.

*During the French and Indian War, George Washington—who later became the first president of the United States— fought with the British against the French and Indians in the Ohio Country.*

*Chief Pontiac believed that Indians should not follow European customs or use European goods.*

## PONTIAC'S REBELLION: 1763–1764

Chief Pontiac, an Ottawa Indian, was born in northwestern Ohio around 1720. He and his people had been friendly with the French traders. At the end of the French and Indian War, after the French were forced to leave the Ohio Country, Pontiac encouraged all Ohio Indians to attack British forts and settlements. He tried to convince all Indians that it would be best for them to return to the way they used to live, before Europeans arrived. Leaders from other Indian groups—including the Shawnee, Huron, Miami, and Delaware—liked his ideas. But without help from the French, they could not keep up their raids on British forts.

## MORAVIAN MISSIONARIES: 1772

David Zeisberger and John Heckewelder were Moravian missionaries. A missionary is a person sent by his or her religious group to spread the teachings of that religion. These **Protestant** missionaries left Moravia, a region in the former Eastern European country of Czechoslovakia, to **convert** Indians to Christianity. They arrived in Ohio in 1772 with Delaware Indians from Pennsylvania. Once in Ohio, the missionaries set up villages. Their first village, named Schoenbrunn, was on the Tuscarawas River. Nearby, there was a similar village called Gnadenhutten. The missionaries believed that the Delaware could keep their traditional **customs** and at the same time accept the Moravian Christian teachings, which were similar to Quaker beliefs.

# The Gnadenhutten Massacre

During the Revolutionary War (1775–1783), a number of Delaware Indians who had been **converted** by Moravian missionaries stayed neutral. They did not help the British or the Americans. Because of this, neither the American soldiers nor the British trusted them. In 1782, toward the end of the war, American soldiers murdered nearly one hundred innocent Christian Indian men, women, and children at the town of Gnadenhutten. The soldiers wrongly believed that the Indians were responsible for an attack on a nearby settlement. The killing of these peaceful Indians in their village became known as the Gnadenhutten Massacre.

When Colonel William Crawford, a settler who was known for his raids against Indians, tried to defeat the Wyandot Indians in Upper Sandusky in 1782, he was captured, tortured, and burned at the stake as payback for this massacre.

## Lord Dunmore's War: October 10, 1774

The Shawnee leader Cornstalk moved to Ohio from Pennsylvania with his family around 1730. They settled near the Scioto River. When he grew older, his skill as a speaker led him to become a leader.

In 1774, the governor of Virginia, Lord Dunmore, led troops north from Virginia to help the settlers defend the land they had taken from the Indians. In response, Cornstalk gathered warriors from around Ohio. They fought Lord Dunmore and his Virginia troops at the Battle of Point Pleasant along the Ohio River. Among the Indians killed was Pucksinwah, father of Tecumseh (see page 29). The Wyandot Chief Tarhe and his warriors also fought with Cornstalk at the Battle of Point Pleasant, as did Chief Logan of the Mingo. The British soldiers were

*Chief Tarhe's nickname was "The Crane." Historians think this is because he was very tall and slender.*

victorious, and the Shawnee signed a treaty giving up their right to all land east and south of the Ohio River. Chief Logan did not sign the treaty.

*In his native language, Cornstalk's name was Keigh-tugh-qua.*

Even after the Shawnee signed the treaty, fighting between Indians and settlers continued. In 1777, Cornstalk traveled to Point Pleasant to talk about peace with the settlers. By that time, the colonists had begun fighting the American Revolution against the British. Instead of talking peace, they captured Cornstalk and his son and placed them in jail. When

## Chief Logan's Speech

Chief Logan had been a friend to the settlers until a group of them murdered his entire family in 1774. He became very bitter, and fought many battles after their deaths. After the Battle of Point Pleasant, Logan sent a message that has become famous. In the message, he explained that he was left without relatives, and that there was no one left to remember him.

*"I appeal to [ask of] any white man to say that he ever entered Logan's cabin, but I gave him meat; that he ever came naked, but I clothed him ... During the course of the long and bloody war Logan remained idle [quiet] in his cabin, an advocate for [supporter of] peace. Such was my love for the whites that my countrymen pointed as they passed and said, 'Logan is the friend of white men.' I had even thought to have lived with you but for the injuries of one man. Colonel Cresap, the last spring, in cold blood and unprovoked [without cause], murdered all the relations of Logan, not even sparing my women and children ... Who is there to mourn for Logan? Not one."*

word came that an American soldier had been killed, supposedly by the Shawnee, an angry group of Americans murdered Cornstalk and his son. This incident, among others, led other Indians to fight against the Americans during the American Revolutionary War.

## THE REVOLUTIONARY WAR: 1775–1783

When the Revolutionary War erupted in 1775 between the American colonists and the British, Ohio's Indians saw a chance to win back some of their original territory. The Shawnee, Miami, Ottawa, and Wyandot gave the British their support, hoping to rid their land of American settlers.

The Delaware Indians, who lived near present-day Coshocton, first sided with the Americans. The Delaware chief at that time was White Eyes (Koquethagechton). White Eyes attended the Continental Congress—a group of people who spoke for the Americans—as a representative of the Delaware people. He agreed to help the Americans against Britain in the war. He even asked the Americans to let the Delaware Indians become a state in the new United States. When White Eyes died in 1778, while serving as a guide for the American troops in the **Ohio Country,** most Delaware then gave their support to the British.

In 1776, White Eyes spent several months in Philadelphia, Pennsylvania, talking to members of the Continental Congress. He talked to them in this room, the Assembly Room in Independence Hall.

When the revolution ended in 1783, the Americans had won. The Ohio Indians had again chosen the wrong side. As more and more white settlers moved westward to Ohio, they pushed Indians off their land and out of their villages. They cleared the woodlands for farmland and cities. Many treaties were made between the Indians and the settlers, but the settlers often broke them and took more Indian land. For example, by 1785 there were 12,000 white settlers living on Indian land in Ohio in spite of treaties which said they should not be there. Tensions rose, and battles broke out across the territory. Undeterred by their recent loss in the revolution, most of Ohio's Indians continued to fight against the settlers.

## TECUMSEH AND HARMAR'S DEFEAT: OCTOBER 1790

Tecumseh, the son of a Shawnee war chief, was born near Xenia, Ohio, on March 9, 1768. His name means "Panther Passing Across the Sky." He was given this name because a meteor, or shooting star, crossed the sky when he was born. When Tecumseh was six years old, his father Pucksinwah died in battle during Lord Dunmore's War (see page 26).

As Tecumseh grew, his older brother Chiksika taught him how to become a warrior. He was a good marksman, and his brother took him on hunting trips. Tecumseh, however, possessed a special talent

*Tecumseh believed in violent **resistance** to white settlers who settled on Indian land.*

*Little Turtle helped **negotiate** the Treaty of Greenville.*

*Although originally a rich man, General Arthur St. Clair died in poverty after the U.S. government failed to pay him back for the money he loaned them while serving as governor of the Northwest Territory.*

as a leader. As an adult, he worked to bring many tribes together. He knew they could be more powerful if they joined together than if they acted alone.

In 1790, Tecumseh and his warriors joined Little Turtle (of the Miami) and Blue Jacket (of the Shawnee) to fight General Josiah Harmar. Harmar had been ordered by the United States government to destroy the major Indian villages in the area. Harmar's army was made up of mostly untrained militiamen, and the Indians soundly defeated them. Harmar lost 183 men.

## St. Clair's Defeat: November 4, 1791

Harmar's defeat only made the Americans more determined to strengthen their hold on the **Ohio Country.** Arthur St. Clair, governor of the **Northwest Territory,** decided to take matters into his own hands. In November of 1791, his troops arrived near several Miami villages. On November 4, the Indian leaders Little Turtle, Blue Jacket, and Tecumseh led Shawnee, Miami, Delaware, and Ottawa warriors against St. Clair and his soldiers. After three hours of fighting, the American soldiers that had not been killed or wounded retreated, leaving the Indians victorious.

## The Battle of Fallen Timbers: August 20, 1794

After the Indians defeated General St. Clair, President Washington sent General "Mad" Anthony Wayne to the Northwest Territory. General Wayne built many more forts. When Little Turtle heard about Wayne's reputation in battle, he became afraid that his warriors would be defeated. He urged the Ohio Indians to agree to terms of peace, but finally

turned over his leadership to the Shawnee leader Blue Jacket, who wanted to fight. Blue Jacket led the Shawnee, Wyandot, and Delaware in a

*Ohio's Indians lost the Battle of Fallen Timbers to General Anthony Wayne.*

raid on General Wayne's men at the Battle of Fallen Timbers on August 20, 1794. The Indians hoped that the British would join them in their fight against the Americans, but they did not. The battle was short, and the Indians were overpowered by American troops. With no support from the British, the Indians had to make a choice about whether or not they would continue to fight.

## TREATY OF GREENVILLE: AUGUST 3, 1795

One year later, on August 3, 1795, more than one thousand Indians from twelve Indian nations, including the Miami, Wyandot, Shawnee, Ottawa, and Delaware, met with General Wayne to sign the Treaty of Greenville. They agreed to give up their land in the Ohio Valley, and were sent to live in northern Ohio in the Black Swamp. This was an area the settlers did not want because it was too wet to settle or farm. The treaty permitted the Indians to hunt on lands that were not developed by the settlers. The Indians gave up their lands east of the Cuyahoga River, and south and east from Fort Laurens to Fort Recovery (map page 22).

*This photograph of the Treaty of Greenville, signed in 1795, shows the signatures or marks of General Anthony Wayne (top), Chief Little Turtle (second from bottom), and other Indian leaders.*

The Indians were given $20,000 worth of goods, which were divided among all of the Ohio nations and Indian settlements.

The Treaty of Greenville began the removal of Ohio's Indians to **reservations** in the American West. Nearly all Indians who had lived in the **Ohio Country** were forced to move west within 40 years.

Tecumseh did not attend the signing of the treaty, and he did not move to the portion of land that the treaty set aside. He did not believe that the land could belong to anyone. He did not want to give up his home and traditions just to please the settlers. He continued to fight.

## Tecumseh's Letter

In 1810, Tecumseh wrote a letter to William Henry Harrison. Harrison was at the time the territorial governor of the **Indiana Territory,** and he later became the ninth president of the United States. In his letter, Tecumseh wrote: "Sell a country! Why not sell the air, the clouds, and the great sea, as well as the earth? Did not the Great Spirit make them all for the use of his children?"

*Tenskwatawa, also known as the Prophet, was Tecumseh's brother. His name means "he who opens the door."*

## TECUMSEH'S CONFEDERATION

Tecumseh began to unite Ohio's Indians to fight against the settlers. His younger brother, Tenskwatawa, may have inspired this idea. Tenskwatawa was known as the Prophet. He had a vision, or dream. In this dream, the Prophet met the Great Spirit. The Great Spirit told him to return to his Indian ways and to give up the ways of the Europeans. The Prophet gave up alcohol and convinced other Indians to do the same. He realized that the alcohol provided by French and British traders weakened the Indians' beliefs. He wanted his people to return to their old **customs.**

Tecumseh and the Prophet built a town called Prophetstown on the Tippecanoe River in Indiana. The brothers hoped all of Ohio's Indians

*More than 100 Indians and settlers, led by Tenskwatawa and Harrison, died at the Battle of Tippecanoe.*

*William Henry Harrison built his fame on the role he played in the Battle of Tippecanoe.*

would come to the new village. They realized that together, the different nations would be stronger than they would be apart. Tecumseh left the town on a six-month trip to ask Indians living in the southern United States to move to Prophetstown. While he was gone, William Henry Harrison planned a raid on the town. Few Indians were killed because they hid in the woods, but Prophetstown

*Tecumseh was killed during the Battle of Thames, which was a part of the War of 1812. After Tecumseh's death, most of the remaining Indian warriors lost heart and left the battlefield.*

was destroyed along with Tecumseh's dream of a strong Indian nation to protect the land.

After the destruction of Prophetstown, most Indians returned to where they had come from. Tecumseh tried to enlist the help of the British, and fought with them against Harrison during the **War of 1812,** but it was his last attempt to protect his land. Harrison's soldiers killed Tecumseh at the Battle of Thames in Ontario, Canada, in 1813. After Tecumseh died, Indians in Ohio no longer fought back. They were forced to move west to **reservations.**

## FORCED REMOVAL

In the years following the signing of the Treaty of Greenville, Ohio's Indians were forced to move west. In 1818, the Miami moved first to Indiana, and then later to Kansas. In 1829, the Delaware left Ohio to move to Kansas. In 1831, the remaining Ohio Shawnee moved to reservations in Oklahoma and Kansas. The Mingo were also forced to move west in that year. They moved first to Kansas, then to Oklahoma. The last of the Ottawa

## Wyandot Warriors

The Wyandot were known as very fierce warriors.

General Wayne once instructed one of his men to capture a resident of the Indian village at Upper Sandusky so he could learn their plans. The man replied that he "could bring in a prisoner, but not from Sandusky, because there are none but Wyandots at Sandusky and they would not be taken alive."

Even the fierce Wyandot warriors, however, could not stop the United States government from forcing them to leave their homeland.

## Tecumseh's Words

*"So live your life that the fear of death can never enter your heart. Trouble no one about their religion; respect others in their view, and demand that they respect yours. Love your life, perfect your life, beautify all things in your life. Seek to make your life long and its purpose in the service of your people. Prepare a noble death song for the day when you go over the great divide. Always give a word or a sign of salute when meeting or passing a friend, even a stranger, when in a lonely place. Show respect to all people and grovel to [beg of] none. When you arise in the morning give thanks for the food and for the joy of living. If you see no reason for giving thanks, the fault lies only in yourself. Abuse [hurt] no one and no thing, for abuse turns the wise ones to fools and robs the spirit of its vision. When it comes your time to die, be not like those whose hearts are filled with the fear of death, so that when their time comes they weep and pray for a little more time to live their lives over again in a different way. Sing your death song and die like a hero going home."*

were forced from Ohio in 1833. They joined other Ottawa people who had left earlier for Kansas. In 1843, the remaining Wyandot were forced to move to Wyandotte County, Kansas. They were the last tribe to leave Ohio.

*Taken away from their traditional lands and forced to move to a new place, many of Ohio's Indians came to depend on the federal government for food. This photograph shows government troops passing out sacks of flour to Indians newly arrived in Oklahoma.*

# Ohio Indians Today

**O**hio, with an American Indian population of 24,486, ranks 25th among the states in the number of Indians living there. Unlike states in the west, or even in neighboring states, there are no **reservations** in Ohio. The government does not recognize these people to be Indians. They receive no federal assistance like those who live on reservations. Some of Ohio's Indians have protested to the government about this issue.

*In recent years, Ohio Indians have taken to the streets in order to ask the government to address their concerns.*

*The Native American Indian Center in central Ohio offers art classes and job counseling, and gives help to those in need.*

Ohio's Indian population today is made up of many different Indian groups. Some of these groups, such as the Shawnee, Delaware, and Miami, have historical roots in Ohio. Others belong to groups that did not traditionally live in Ohio, such as the Navajo, Choctaw, and Cherokee. Many of the Indians who live in Ohio today are the descendants of those who came to Ohio during the late 1800s. They came from **reservations** looking for better jobs. Many of them were hired to work factory jobs in steel mines in towns like Toledo, Cleveland, and Youngstown.

The Native American Indian Center of Central Ohio in Columbus helps area residents learn about their past. According to this group's records, more than 10,000 Indians from tribes throughout the United States live in central Ohio alone. The center offers classes in drumming, native languages, regalia (traditional clothing) making, and crafts. Elders, storytellers, and dancers from different tribes help teach younger people about their **heritage.** Powwows, or celebrations, are held several times a year. Social services to help those in need are also available at the center.

*Today, many Ohio Indians continue to dance as their ancestors did hundreds of years ago. Dancing is a link to their past. This Ottawa girl is dancing at an annual festival.*

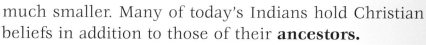

## PRESENT-DAY BELIEFS AND PRACTICES

The number of Indians in Ohio who practice their traditional beliefs varies, just as it does in other **cultures.** Some present-day Indian leaders in Ohio think as many as 85 percent keep their traditional Indian beliefs. Others think the numbers are much smaller. Many of today's Indians hold Christian beliefs in addition to those of their **ancestors.**

Brian Day, who is a member of the Piqua Sept of Ohio Shawnee Tribe, says many of his fellow Shawnee trace their roots to early Ohio peoples. The members get together each season to celebrate their heritage. "Our gatherings are based on the seasons: preplanting, planting, harvest, and winter. We have dances, feasts, raffles, tribal council meetings, recreational events, and activities for children. These are similar to what other cultures include in their festivals," Day says. Indians wear traditional dress, called regalia, during some of the ceremonies, especially during the Green Corn Dance and the Bread Dance. Special foods, like corn soup and pemmican bread (special bread

*Pemmican is usually made from berries, honey, crushed seeds or nuts, and dried beef, venison, or buffalo.*

*Each year, a theater group in Chillicothe, Ohio, recreates the story of Tecumseh on a huge, outdoor stage. Every summer, thousands of people learn about the struggle of the Shawnee people and their history in the state of Ohio.*

made with dried meat and grains) are often served. "We go over our history and the things that connect us to the past. It is a time for elders to talk to the young ones," Day explains. "We teach our children to respect creation and nature."

"Hollywood has changed what white people think about us. There are **stereotypes,** but we are ordinary people," Day explains. Stereotypes are ideas about a whole group of people that are not true. Day adds that two words that came from the movies and are not part of Indian ways in any **culture** are "squaw" and "how."

Logan Sharp is a Mekoce (pronounced mek-OH-chee) Shawnee Indian who lives in Wilmington, Ohio. He was a chief until his retirement in 2002. His Shawnee grandmother was the "keeper of traditions" in his family. She remembered the stories handed down to her and told them to the children in the family. Sharp

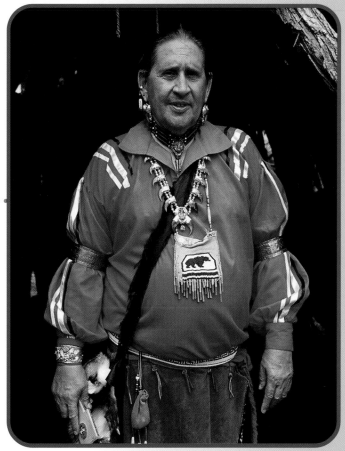

*Present-day Indians in Ohio work to keep their **heritage** alive by celebrating in the clothing of their ancestors.*

learned much of what he knows of his tribe's history and traditions from his grandmother. Sharp says that children are also taught by example. "Spiritual lessons are lived every day," he says.

"We have jobs, eat at McDonald's, and wear blue jeans," explains Sharp, who works as an electrician. Sharp traces his Shawnee roots back to 1812. His family was one of the few Shawnee families that stayed in Ohio after the Treaty of Greenville. They remained after the United States government forced most of Ohio's Indians to western **reservations.** They stayed to take care of the Indians who could not make the trip west. Others stayed to look after the sacred burial grounds of their **ancestors.**

## Indian Gathering

Each summer, the Ohio Historical Society plans American Indian gatherings at Fort Ancient and Flint Ridge. These are times to learn about the music, villages, medicines, and other traditions of Indians who live and lived in Ohio. You can find out more information about these gatherings by contacting the Ohio Historical Society in Columbus.

Logan Sharp joins other Indians during special ceremonies throughout the year. He says that the birth of a child is cause for members to celebrate. In his Shawnee tradition, another important ceremony occurs when children receive their tribal name, at around age thirteen. "Everyone comes together, even from other tribes. It is a passage in becoming an adult member," Sharp explains. Wedding ceremonies also follow the Indian traditions.

In the Lumbee Nation, children today are given earth names at birth. Tom Netz, the storyteller and band chief of the United Lumbee Great Lakes Band in northwestern Ohio, says children are "gifted" with, or given, an earth name sometime between the ten days before or after their birth. "The father, mother, or grandparents can choose the name. We look within the earth for a unique name," he explains. If a name is not given at birth, older children or adults can be named later. Netz's tribe holds four special ceremonies each year. They occur around new moon cycles. "That is when each family brings traditional foods."

*This Lumbee child, dressed in traditional clothing, is learning about his heritage and the history of his people.*

Today, Ohio's Indians are proud of their **heritage.** They keep the traditions of their past alive for themselves and future generations.

## Ohio's Indian Words

Many Ohioans don't realize that some of the words they use or see every day are Indian words. Look around you: it is easy to see the many contributions that Indian words have made to the state of Ohio.

| WORD/PLACE NAME | MEANING |
| --- | --- |
| Ashtabula | "fish river" |
| Auglaize | "fallen timbers" |
| Coshocton | "black bear town" |
| Cuyahoga | "crooked" |
| Erie | "cat" |
| Geauga | "raccoon" |
| Hocking | "bottle" |
| Mahoning | "at the salt lick" |
| Maumee | "muddy water" |
| Muskingum | "a town by the river" |
| Ohio | "great" or "beautiful river" |
| Pataskala | "salt lick" |
| Sandusky | "water within water pools" |
| Scioto | "deer" |
| Tuscarawas | "open mouth" |

# Map of Ohio

Lake Erie

Toledo
Napoleon
Cleveland • Orange
Sandusky
Oberlin
Fremont
Cuyahoga R.
Niles
Lordstown
Youngstown
Akron
Ohio City
Ada
Mansfield
Orrville • Canton
Grand Lake
Wapakoneta
Delaware Lake
Gambier
Marysville
Quincy
Delaware
Minster
Dublin
Zanesville
Columbus
New Concord
Quaker City
Millersport
New Carlisle
Dayton
Xenia
Circleville
Athens
Lebanon
North Bend
Hillsboro
Zaleski
Cincinnati
Point Pleasant
Wellston
Ripley
Ohio River

Maumee River
Sandusky River
Scioto River
Muskingum River
Great Miami River
Ohio River

N
W E
S

0        50 mi.

| | |
|---|---|
| ✪ | Capital |
| • | City |
| ~ | River |
| — | State line |

Wisconsin
Michigan
Pennsylvania
Illinois
Indiana
Ohio
Delaware
West Virginia
Kentucky
Virginia

# Timeline

| | |
|---|---|
| **13,000–7,000 B.C.E.** | Paleo-Indians live in **Ohio country.** |
| **8000–500 B.C.E.** | Ohio Archaic Indians use the atlatl for hunting. They also gather plants and trade flint with other groups. |
| **800 B.C.E.–C.E. 100** | Early Woodland Indians known as the Adena build burial mounds and earthworks. |
| **C.E. 100–500** | Middle Woodland Indians known as the Hopewell arrive and continue to build mounds and earthworks. |
| **500–1200** | Late Woodland people begin growing corn in addition to other crops, and use bows and arrows to hunt. |
| **900–1550** | Late **Prehistoric** Indians called the Fort Ancient people build permanent settlements in Ohio and farm, hunt, and fish. Their fate is unknown. |
| **1650–1843** | **Historic** period: tribes such as the Delaware and Shawnee enter Ohio and remain until they are removed to **reservations** in Oklahoma and Kansas by the federal government. |
| **1754** | The **French and Indian War** begins in the New World between Great Britain and France with its Indian **allies.** |
| **1763** | France loses all of its land rights in America after losing the French and Indian War and signing the Treaty of Paris. |
| **1763** | Chief Pontiac and other Indian supporters wage a series of battles, called Pontiac's Rebellion, against the British. |
| **1768** | Tecumseh is born near present-day Xenia. |
| **1772** | Moravian missionaries build the town of Schoenbrunn in northeastern Ohio. |
| **1774** | Lord Dunmore's War takes place along the Ohio River; Tecumseh's father dies in battle. |
| **1775–1783** | The American Revolutionary War takes place. |
| **1782** | The Gnadenhutten Massacre occurs. |
| **1794** | General Wayne overtakes Indians at Battle of Fallen Timbers. |
| **1795** | Most Ohio Indian leaders sign the Treaty of Greenville, giving up most of their land claims in the **Northwest Territory.** |
| **1803** | Ohio becomes a state. |
| **1812** | The **War of 1812** begins. |
| **1843** | The Wyandot, the last of the Ohio Indians, leave for reservations in the west. |

# Glossary

**Algonquian** group of American Indian languages spoken by many Indians living in Canada, New England, and the Great Lakes region

**ally** person or group who agrees to help another person or group. An alliance is an agreement between allies.

**ancestor** one from whom an individual has descended

**archaeologist** person who studies history through the remains of people and what they have made or built

**artifact** something created by humans for a practical purpose during a certain time period

**astronomer** scientist who studies the stars

**Beaver Wars** series of struggles that took place between 1650 and 1700 between the Iroquois (who had come from the east) and the Indians already living in the Ohio Country. They were fighting over control of Ohio's hunting grounds.

**breechcloth** piece of cloth worn around the hips as a covering

**clan** group of people who share a common relative who lived in the past

**consequence** effect

**convert** to change a person's religious beliefs

**culture** ideas, skills, arts, and a way of life of a certain people at a certain time

**custom** something a person or group does that had been done for a long time and became a habit

**enclosure** closed-in area

**epidemic** when a group of people have all been affected by an illness or disease

**excavate** to uncover by digging

**extinct** no longer living

**French and Indian War** (1754–1763) war fought between France and Great Britain over control of North America

**game** animal hunted for food or sport

**germ warfare** purposeful spreading of germs to make an enemy sick or die

**heritage** something that comes from one's ancestors

**hide** animal skin

**historic** time when history was recorded or written down

**Ice Age** period of colder climate when much of North America was covered by thick glaciers

**Indiana Territory** during the early 1800s, land that included Illinois, Wisconsin, most of Indiana, eastern Minnesota, and western Michigan

**land bridge** land connecting Alaska and Siberia during the last Ice Age when the sea level was much lower

**longhouse** long, rectangular-shaped home lived in by many Indians at once. Longhouses had frames made of wooden poles, and were covered by bark or animal skins.

**mammoth** prehistoric relative of today's elephant

**mastodon** prehistoric relative of today's elephant. Mastodons were shorter and stockier than mammoths.

**mica** type of stone that comes in many colors and flakes easily into very thin slices

**negotiate** to talk with others and arrive at an agreement

**nomad** hunter who moves from place to place following the herds of wild animals

**Northwest Territory** in the late 1700s, the territory made up of present-day Ohio, Indiana, Illinois, and parts of Michigan and Wisconsin

**obsidian** black volcanic glass

**Ohio Country** roughly, the area of modern-day Ohio, eastern Indiana, western Pennsylvania, and northwestern West Virginia

**parallel** two or more lines, set close together, that run in the same direction and never touch or meet

**pelt** skin of a furry animal

**plaza** public square in a village or town

**prehistoric** time before history was recorded or written down

**projectile point** pointed stone object, such as a spear head, that was made to be thrown through the air

**Protestant** type of Christian

**refugee** person who flees from a war or other danger

**reservation** tract of public land set aside for use by American Indians

**resistance** ability to avoid being affected by a disease or illness; also, struggling against something or someone

**resource** something that is available to take care of a need; there are natural and human-made resources

**shellfish** animal that lives in the water and has no skeleton, but which has an outer shell to protect it

**stereotype** unfair judgment about a person or a group of people

**sundial** instrument that shows the time of day using shadows

**tap** to poke through the bark of a maple tree so that sap flows out; the sap is then used to make maple syrup

**War of 1812** (1812–1814) war between the United States and Great Britain; Great Britain was supporting Indian raids against settlers in the Ohio Country

# More Books to Read

Cavan, Seamus. *Daniel Boone and the Opening of the Ohio Country.* Broomall, Penn.: Chelsea House Publishers, 1991.

Flanagan, Alice K. *The Shawnee.* Danbury, Conn.: Scholastic Library Publishing, 2000.

Gregson, Susan R. *Tecumseh: Shawnee Leader.* Minnetonka, Minn.: Capstone Press, 2003.

Howes, Kathi. *The Ottawa.* Vero Beach, FL.: Rourke Publishing, 1992.

Marsh, Carole. *Ohio Indian Dictionary for Kids!* Peachtree City, GA.: Gallopade International, 1996.

# Index

# About the Author

Marcia Schonberg is a lifelong resident of Ohio. She writes regularly for daily newspapers and regional and national *magazines*. Her list of books includes the children's book *B is for Buckeye*. A graduate of Ohio State University, Schonberg now makes her home in Lexington with her husband Bill.